IS THAT A CAT?

TIM HAMILTON

Holiday House / New York

For Ted and Betsy Lewin,
a couple of great teachers

HOLIDAY HOUSE is registered in the U.S. Patent and Trademark Office.
Printed and Bound in April 2015 at Toppan Leefung, DongGuan City, China.
The artwork was created with pen and ink,
watercolors and digital tools.
www.holidayhouse.com
First Edition
1 3 5 7 9 10 8 6 4 2

Library of Congress Cataloging-in-Publication Data
Hamilton, Tim, author, illustrator.
Is that a cat? / Tim Hamilton. — First edition.
pages cm. — (I like to read)
Summary: Several animals, an elf, and a bird-watcher are searching
for different things, but find each other—and a party—instead.
ISBN 978-0-8234-3384-1 (hardcover)
[1. Animals—Fiction. 2. Parties—Fiction.] I. Title.
PZ7.H18265881s 2015
[E]—dc23
2014032159

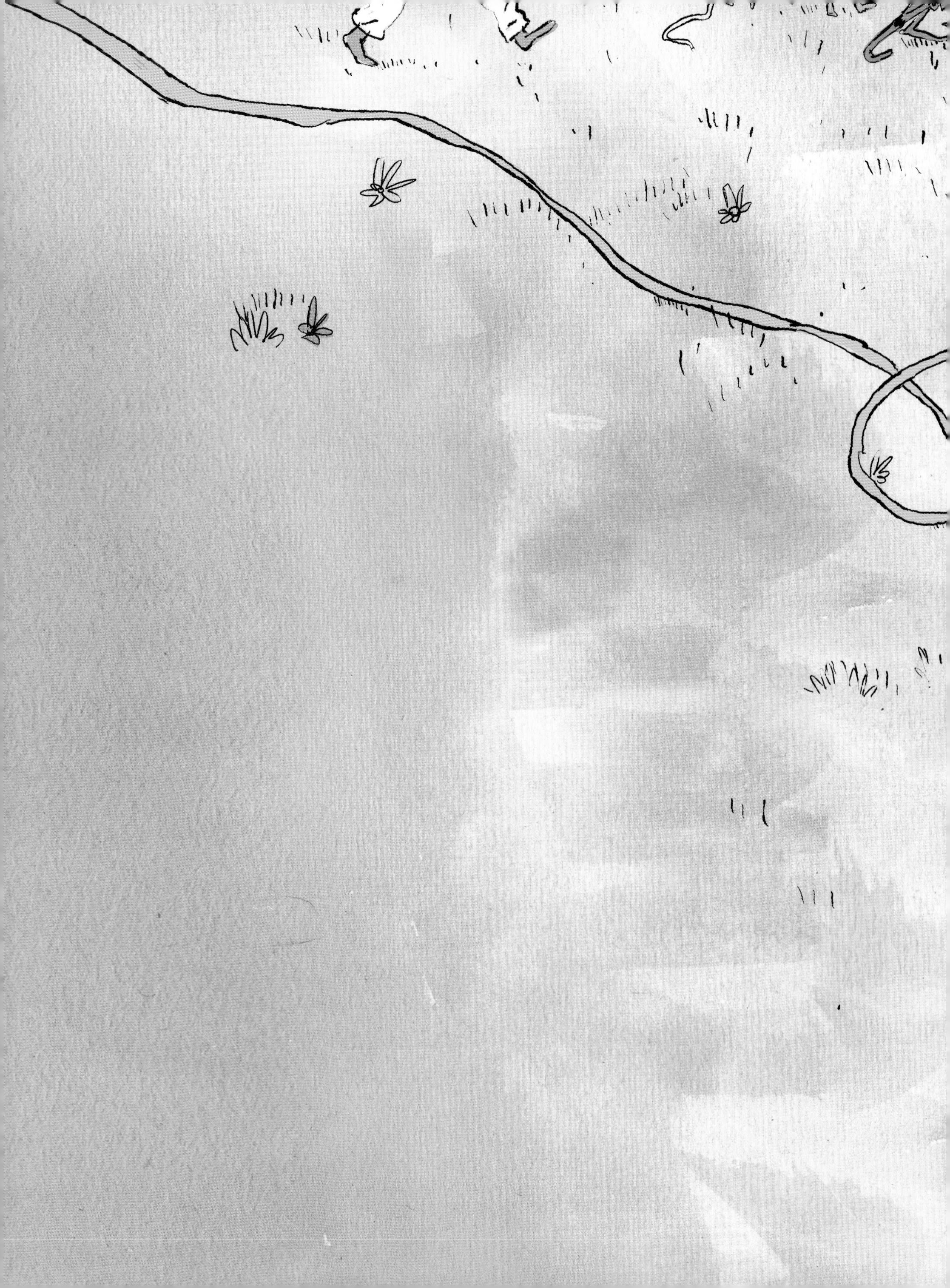

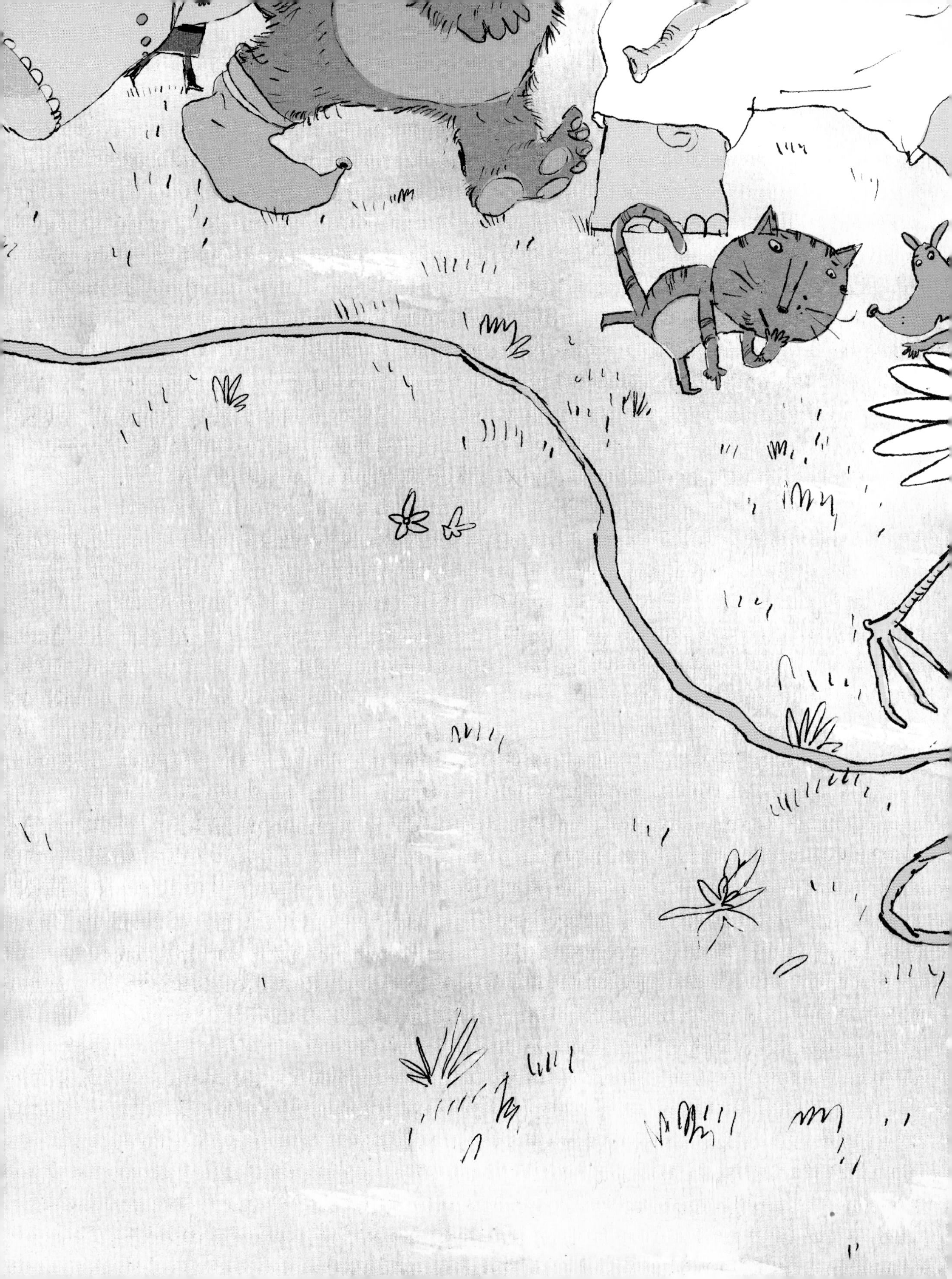

Also by Tim Hamilton

The Big Fib

An I Like to Read® Book

"Rare will be the kid who doesn't get
a kick out of Hamilton's huge-headed, walleyed,
and good-intentioned characters."
—*Booklist*

But!

"This title has much to engage readers:
frequent page-ending pauses of the title
conjunction "but"; humorous plot twists; quirky,
cartoon characterizations; and friendly,
neighborhood pirates."
—*School Library Journal*

"This tale of pirate foolishness
is great good fun."
—*Kirkus Reviews*